KILLER, the OUTRAGEOUS HAWK
By Bonnie Robison

Illustrated By Rob Sprattler
Designed By Rolf Zillmer

HIGH POINT BOOKS

AN ELK GROVE BOOK

 CHILDRENS PRESS, CHICAGO

Library of Congress Cataloging in Publication Data

Robison, Bonnie.
  Killer, the outrageous hawk.

  SUMMARY: A fourteen-year-old boy raises
a baby hawk but finally decides to let it go free.
  "An Elk Grove book."
  "High point book."
(1. Hawks-Fiction) I. Sprattler, Rob illus.
II. Title.
PZ10.3.R612Ki   636.6'869 (Fic)   74-8445
ISBN 0-516-07630-2

  2 3 4 5 6 7 8 9 10 11 12 13 14 15 R 81 80 79 78 77 76 75

To my family and to the best friend Randy ever had.

With special thanks to Doug Roller and his hawk for their assistance with the illustrations.

Chapter 1

Mom said her first impression of Killer was indelible. That's the way Mom talks, with words like indelible. But she was right about Killer, because he sure was a funny-looking bird when I brought him home that first day.

My friend Ron and I had found a new sport—cliff-climbing. It all started because we liked to explore the hills behind my house. That's one place you can go to think without everyone telling you to clean your room, or finish your homework, or finish a million other things.

Sometimes we camped overnight. Mom wouldn't let me at first because she said I was only fourteen. But finally she decided it was safe because my dog Lucky always went with us. Lucky is a long-legged beagle who likes me better than anything in the world, except maybe eating. He really didn't amount to much as a camp watchdog, but Mom didn't know that.

The day I found the baby hawk, we were testing my new cliff hook that I made in metal shop at school. I copied it from a picture in a mountain-climbing book I was reading. Barney Cooper laughed when he saw the hook. He's a big guy who thinks he knows everything just because he plays varsity basketball.

"Randy, how can you climb a cliff with that thing? It's nothing but a bunch of hooks welded together with a rope tied to one end. Bet you couldn't climb a cliff anyway, you're so skinny."

Several guys in shop laughed with Barney, but I was used to that. Everybody said I had a wild imagination, even my parents, and maybe they were right. But I glared at Barney anyway because it made me fighting mad to be called skinny, and he knew it.

The cliff hook worked really neat. We were able to explore some cliffs we couldn't even get to before. We anchored the hook to something solid at the top of a cliff and let ourselves down over the edge by hanging on the rope and bracing our feet against the bank. Sometimes we threw the hook over the top and climbed up. Climbing was hard and pretty scary. Now that I think about it, we're lucky we didn't break our necks.

At the foot of this one cliff we found the dead hawk. Its feathers were scattered like it had tried to fly. Lucky was barking his head off.

"It's been shot!" Ron looked around for a hunter.

Nobody was in sight. I looked up and spotted something strange high above our heads.

"Look! Is that a nest?" I asked. "I'm going up."

It was a nest all right, the craziest one I ever saw. It was about the size of a dishpan, hanging on a little ledge. Nothing seemed to be holding it up.

Hand over hand, I inched my way up the rope. All the time dirt and rocks were falling on me from the top of the cliff, but I kept going. Finally, I could look into the nest. There sat this goofy-looking bird, staring back at me, eyeball to eyeball.

He was about as big as a young chicken and covered with gray fuzz. Out of one end of the giant ball of fuzz stuck his head with a curved beak and wild black eyes. Out of the other end came his chickenlike feet, ending in hooked claws a half-inch long.

I didn't know whether to laugh or get the heck out of there. I looked again, and wondered how a bird could look so mean and so lonesome at the same time. Carefully, I picked him up and cradled him with one arm against my chest.

As soon as I started down, I knew I was in trouble. Now I had only one hand to hold the rope. I tried to brace myself against the cliff, but the dirt kept crumbling away under my feet. Several times I slipped and dangled in midair.

About the time I was sorry I'd started the whole thing, I shot a glance at the bird. He snuggled closer against me like he trusted me.

"Nutty bird thinks I'm his mother," I muttered, and I knew I just *had* to make it down. By the time I dropped to the ground, the sweat was running down my face.

Ron's brown eyes popped. "Wow!" he gasped. "What're you gonna do with him, Randy?"

I pushed my hair back out of my eyes. "That must have been the mother hawk that was killed. I couldn't leave the baby there to die, could I?"

Ron shrugged. "I guess not, but—"

"But what?" I stared at him. "Maybe I'll keep him."

"But your dad won't let you keep him, that's what! Besides, what do you know about raising a hawk?"

"Nothing," I had to admit, "but wouldn't he be a neat pet?"

Ron thought about that and grinned. "Yeah."

I got excited and started talking a mile a minute about what I could do with the bird. "I've heard that people hunt with hawks. Wouldn't that be far out?"

Ron gave me this steady look. Then he shook his head. "I've seen you have a lot of crazy ideas, Randy, but you've really done it this time."

I didn't answer. There it was again. Maybe even Ron thought I was nuts. "Let's start back," I said.

We tramped through the high grass and weeds. Winter

rains had left the hills mossy green, and even the trails made by hikers and motorcycle scramblers the summer before were almost covered over. The spring sun felt warm and welcome on my damp head. I ran my fingers through my hair, so maybe Mom wouldn't tell me again that I needed a haircut.

I wrapped the baby bird in my jacket and tried not to jog as I walked. I was glad Ron was a few feet ahead of me, so I could have a chance to think. What would I tell the folks? I knew my twelve-year-old sister Leslee would like him. She liked all animals, even things girls are supposed to be afraid of.

Leslee and I had brought home stray animals before, and Mom and Dad were usually cool about letting us keep them. But maybe Ron was right. After all, a hawk is pretty weird.

I looked at the bird. The piercing eyes were fixed on my face, still staring. I remembered reading that hawks were cold-blooded killers, and I began to believe it.

As we got closer to my house, I could see Dad's car in the driveway, and my stomach flipped over. That meant I wouldn't be able to talk to Mom first. Just my luck!

Ron said goodbye and hurried on home. As I sneaked into the garage to put away my hook and rope, Leslee came around the corner in her usual jeans and sweatshirt.

"Hi, Luck," she said and dropped to hug the dog. Lucky

12 wagged his tail and licked her face. I could feel her looking at me. "Randy, what've you got?"

"Shhh, Les, not so loud," I warned. I unwrapped the bird so she could see. "It's a baby hawk. I found it left in the nest. The mother hawk had been killed."

She caught her breath, then giggled softly. "He's funny, but he's nice." She picked him up and held him lightly. "Do you think we can keep him?" she asked.

Already it was "we." At least Leslee was on my side. We found a cardboard box and an old towel to make a bed, and I carried the box into the house and put it in a corner in my room.

"Dinner's almost ready," Mom called from the kitchen.

"Okay, I'll wash up," I answered as casually as I could.

When we sat down to dinner, I looked up and grinned. "Hi, Dad," I said.

He didn't smile. Uh-oh, that probably meant he'd had a bad day. How was I going to break the news?

2

Chapter

All through dinner I was nervous, but I tried not to show it. I couldn't even look at Leslee. By the time we got to dessert, she couldn't stand it any longer.

"Randy, tell them about the baby hawk," she blurted.

I shot her a dirty look because I was still thinking of a way to break it to Mom and Dad gently. Now it was too late.

Dad turned to me with that "now what?" look on his face. "What baby hawk?"

Helplessly I nodded toward my room. "I have something to show you."

In my room, all four of us stood looking down at the bird. It was so quiet, I could hear my heart thumping.

"I named him 'Killer' because he looks so mean," I said, just for conversation.

"That's the understatement of the year," Mom said. She looked for a second like she might run, but she didn't.

I lifted the bird out of the box and set him down on the hard polished floor. He scrambled to stand up and rocked back and forth before he got his balance. He tried to take a step, put one foot down on top of the other, tripped himself, and collapsed into a heap of fuzz.

We couldn't help laughing. Killer tried several times to walk, but each effort ended the same way. Finally he sighed and sat back on his haunches, then cocked his head at me like it was all my fault. I put him back in his box, since he seemed to feel safer in there.

Back in the living room, Dad sank down on the couch. "Okay, let's have it. Where did you get that thing?"

I swallowed hard and started to explain. Leslee kept interrupting me, and I kept telling her to shut up. When I got to the part about hanging on the rope with one hand and the rocks falling, Dad leaned forward to listen. Mom turned pale.

I stopped and pushed my hair out of my eyes. "Don't you think he's neat, Mom?"

"Sure," she said in a put-on voice, "he's my favorite."

Mom and Dad looked at each other, then back at me. Dad sighed. "I don't suppose you've thought of all the problems of owning a *preying bird?*"

Oh boy, I thought, here it comes. Dad worked for the County Health Department, and he could always think of rules and reasons why I couldn't do things.

"Um, no, I haven't. But can't I keep him?"

Dad shook his head. "I don't think so. A lot depends on

the law. We have to respect the zoning regulations, you know.
Randy, I'd guess taking care of a hawk would be a lot of work.
And you'd have to buy a license."

That stopped me. "A license! What for?"

"It's a state law. There are all sorts of controls on hawks
and falcons. Some of these birds are becoming extinct, for one
thing. I doubt if you know what you're getting into."

"That bird could be a lot of bother," Mom said. "Is this
another project that you'll start, then not follow through?"

I looked down. How could I make them understand? This
was different. I already felt something special for Killer—he
was so tough—and suddenly I knew I wanted to keep him more
than anything I had ever wanted.

"I'll save the money for the license out of my paper route
money. And I'll go to the library and study about hawks after
school. I'll find somebody who can tell me what to do."

But Dad wasn't really listening. "Sure, sure, Randy. How
many times have we heard things like that before?"

I ran to my room, my eyes smarting. Leslee and Lucky
were right behind me.

"I'll help, too," Leslee said. She kneeled beside the bird's
box. Lucky wagged his tail and put his chin in my lap.

Killer had fallen asleep, unaware of the trouble he'd caused
and that he might soon be homeless.

3
Chapter

The next day I hurried through my paper route and pedaled to the library. There weren't many books on *falconry,* but I brought home everything I could find.

Dad checked for me about the zoning and the license, which he said would cost $15. I almost croaked when I heard that, but I didn't let on. I would have to deliver papers for a whole month to pay for a bird license.

"I'll save the money. Please, Dad, give me a chance. If I don't follow through, then the bird goes. Okay?"

Dad nodded. "All right, Randy, the bird can stay as long as you take care of it, and it doesn't make trouble for your mother."

Leslee jumped up and down and Lucky wagged his tail. Dad was okay, but I knew he expected me to lose interest, and he meant what he said about giving up Killer.

Feeding Killer was my biggest problem. When I called the vet, he said to give him cottage cheese, hamburger, and hard-boiled eggs. He told me to stuff food down the bird's throat, but that wasn't exactly easy. Killer snapped at everything put in front of his face, and he bit me several times.

Killer had to be fed five times a day, and it seemed like

he ate all the time. Leslee helped me by feeding him while I delivered papers. We used an eyedropper for water and tweezers for the food. Killer clamped on to the tweezers and hung on, but he managed to swallow the pieces of food that fell into his mouth. He bit the eyedropper so hard I wondered why it didn't break.

"He sure isn't very friendly," said one of my friends who came to see Killer. Slowly, though, we got used to his long beak and short temper. He learned to eat quickly and even to suck the water out of the dropper.

"But he hasn't learned any table manners," Mom complained. She made us feed Killer on the patio so we could hose it off after each meal.

The next time Ron came to see the bird, his mouth fell open. "Wow, he's grown!" The little quills on the underside of his wings were beginning to sprout feathers.

We started betting on how big he would get. I got out my hawk books and whistled. "Some hawks reach a wingspan of four feet. How about that?" It was plain that I would have to do something soon about a cage to keep him in. A cardboard box would never do for a hawk with a four-foot wingspan.

Killer was so funny trying to walk that we wondered how he would ever learn to fly. Dad chuckled, "This kid needs some basic flight training. He'll never get off the ground."

Then I had another problem. Lucky wasn't exactly crazy about a hawk moving in with him. Mom always said about Lucky, "He has the most positive attitude in dogdom. He greets everybody like an avalanche." It was true too.

But Lucky wasn't all that big on weird birds. He didn't try to harm Killer, but he kept an eye on him even when he pretended not to. He would circle the bird a couple of times, then sit down at a safe distance. He made like a tough watchdog, but down inside, I think he was really afraid the hawk would eat his dinner.

About a week after I found him, I took Killer to school to show him off in science class. I packed a clean box with his food and water for the trip.

I was kind of nervous about taking Killer to school because of his nutty bathroom habits. What I mean is, we thought he was box-broken at first because we found his *mutes* as far as ten feet from the box. We figured he simply climbed out to perform his duty. But we found out later that he was able to raise up from inside the box and squirt.

I thought this was very handy of him, but then it dawned on me. I told Ron, "That must be nature's way of keeping the nest clean before the baby birds can fly."

But Killer seemed to know that he should behave himself
at school, and I sure was relieved about that. He knocked 'em
dead. The teacher and the kids crowded around and watched
me feed him. I was afraid that the noise and the strangers
would scare him, but he just stared at them like *they* were
out of place.

Of course Barney wasn't impressed. He just moved away
muttering, "What's so special about a dumb-looking bird?"
Some of the kids who followed Barney around turned away
too. They always did what he did. Barney had to put people
down, one way or another.

But then he said something that turned out to be important
to me. "Randy, you'll probably end up like Old Mack—raising
birds, for goshsakes."

"Old Mack? You mean the hermit out on Railroad Street?"
I had heard the kids talk about him. He was supposed to be
mean.

"Sure, they say he raises hawks and all kinds of creepy
plants. Why don't you go visit him, Randy?" Barney's friends
laughed. They thought everything he said was funny.

But I hardly noticed. My imagination was racing again.
Why not go see Old Mack? He could help me with Killer.

"Maybe I will," I said.

Chapter 4

I felt silly walking down Railroad Street alone carrying Killer in his cardboard box. Nobody would go with me, not even Ron. At the end of the street the sidewalk stopped, and I picked my way down the path to Old Mack's shack across the field.

The shack looked even more dilapidated up close. I almost lost my nerve, until I glanced down at Killer. There he sat gazing around calmly. No sir, nothing bothered this bird, not even hermits. No doubt about it, Killer had a cool head.

I tapped lightly on the warped door, and secretly hoped nobody would answer. "Maybe he's not home," I whispered to Killer and began to plan a fast getaway. No, better knock once more.

My eyes wandered from the rusted hinges across the unpainted boards to the window, which was too dirty to see through. Then I realized that the door had opened a crack, and a hairy face was staring out at me.

"Who are you? What do you want?" his voice boomed.

I almost dropped Killer. Just the sight of Old Mack made me jump. His hair was faded red, and his bushy beard was the same color. The green eyes blazed through red-rimmed

lids. No wonder the kids were scared of him.

"Um, my name is Randy. I live over that way." I pointed with my head. "I found this baby hawk, and I'm trying to raise it. Well, sir, somebody said you knew a lot about hawks, and . . ." My voice faded away.

He didn't say anything, just looked me over from head to foot. Finally his eyes stopped on Killer. "A baby hawk, huh? Well, come on in." The door sagged open.

I hoped he couldn't see my knees wobble as I stepped inside the room. He turned and shuffled over to a bare table by the window. "Bring it here."

Through the junk on the floor, I followed him, thinking it was a good thing Mom couldn't see this house. She thinks *my* room is messy. Books were stacked everywhere. Two dogs sniffed at my heels, and I was glad I'd left Lucky at home.

With gnarled fingers, the old man gently lifted Killer out of the box onto the table. Just like magic, his gruffness disappeared when he touched the bird. For a long time he squinted at Killer, and I wondered if he had forgotten I was there.

"Humph, a red-tailed *tiercel.* Where'd you get him?" He looked at me suspiciously.

I told him about the nest and the mother hawk, glad that I had read about *red-tails* and that I knew the tiercel was the male hawk.

"Humph," again. "Folks shouldn't stick their noses into hawks' business unless they know what they're doing. You say you're gonna raise him?" He said it like he didn't believe me.

"Yes sir, if I can. Do you think he's okay, I mean healthy and everything?"

He shook his shaggy head slowly. "Miracle. Miracle he's alive. Mother hawks protect the young, you know. Keep 'em warm."

I didn't know, but I nodded anyway. My mind raced back and I started to worry. The last few nights we had left Killer outside because Mom said he was too messy to be in the house. I looked around, feeling guilty.

Then I saw the statue of a hawk, sitting on a cork pedestal in the corner. The statue was wearing a *hood,* a fancy leather one with feathers on top. The hood was to keep a hawk calm, I had read.

I walked over to the pedestal to get a better look, and as I came close, the head of the bird moved. I gasped and stepped back. The statue shifted its weight and jingled the bells attached to its feet. It wasn't a statue at all! It was alive.

Deep laughter filled the room. It was Mack breaking up, laughing at my surprise. He was completely different when he laughed.

He chuckled and said, "Meet Vida, my *prairie falcon*
queen."

I was so excited I couldn't say anything. Vida was beautiful.
She was so well trained that she sat quietly on her *perch*. No
wonder he was proud of her.

"Wow, she's something else," I said at last. "Does she
hunt?"

"Vida catches rabbits and small birds and mice. Good
hunter." Mack sure didn't waste any words.

"What are the bells for?" I asked. They made a special
sound, like sleigh bells on a horse, softened by the leather
leash.

"So I can keep track of her," he said, watching me again.

"How do you get her back?"

"Easy," he said. "Trained her to a whistle and *lure,* a piece
of meat on a string."

"Oh." I began to relax, and walked back to the table.
"What shall I feed Killer? That's his name."

"Got to have calcium," he said. "The *eyas* is fed by the
mother and gets pieces of bone in fresh meat."

"Where'll I get calcium?" I figured an eyas must be a
baby bird. I told him about the cottage cheese and eggs and
hamburger.

Mack shrugged. "That's good, but break calcium tablets up in his food. Wild food is best, though. Feed him a live mouse once a week."

That did it! I knew Mom would blow her top if I brought in live mice. "Okay," I said, but I almost choked on the word.

"Hawk has to have wild food for *castings* to clean his stomach. He spits out undigested feathers and fur."

"You sure know a lot about hawks," I said as I put Killer back in his box.

"Birds and I get along fine." Mack looked almost friendly now. "People think I'm funny, but I have a good life with my animals, my books, and my garden."

I hesitated. "Uh, could I come see you again? Maybe I'll try to train Killer."

Old Mack looked at me a minute, like he was deciding if he could trust me. I was afraid I'd gone too far.

Finally he grunted, "Guess so, long as you like birds."

I was surprised at how much I wanted to hear that answer. I ran almost all the way home, eager to tell Mom and Dad and Leslee about Mack. Also I wanted to get started with Killer's training.

That night I lay in bed thinking about falconry. I pictured myself standing in the middle of a field, maybe even at school, and Killer swooping down from the sky to land on my arm.

All the kids were cheering when I fell asleep.

5

Chapter

The first thing I did to train Killer was give a loud whistle when I brought his food. At first he nearly jumped out of his box. When he was scared, he always jumped backward about six inches. The whistle increased the jump to a good foot.

Pretty soon, though, he got used to it and hardly jumped at all. He even learned to connect the whistle with feeding time. In fact, everybody on our side of town knew when Killer was eating.

All the time I was boning up on falconry, Killer slept, grew feathers, and staggered around trying to walk. He cocked his head to listen, sometimes turning his head completely upside down. He cheeped a lot, like an overgrown chicken, especially while he ate.

I bought a live mouse in the pet store later that week and fed it to Killer. I did it away from the house, so Mom wouldn't have to see it. Mostly, though, he ate beef heart, which he liked better than cottage cheese. His claws grew into strong *pounces,* as they are called—the weapons of the hawk. He learned to tear his meat into shreds before he ate it.

"Isn't he getting cute?" Leslee said one day.

"Sure, Les," I groaned. Killer was proud, dignified, and fierce, but not cute.

"Well," she pouted, "what would you call him?"

I thought about that a minute. "I think he's outrageous." I liked the word, and it seemed to fit Killer. The most outrageous thing about him was his eyes. I had read that a hawk's eyesight is eight times better than a man's. That was easy to believe when Killer looked clear through you and out the other side. He learned to crouch his head like a snake ready to strike. It was spooky.

I also found out that hawks have a special system of eyelids. They can blink from bottom to top and side to side. I thought that was really something, and I tried to catch Killer doing the side to side bit, but he was too fast for me.

When the license came in the mail, I made the sound of rolling drums and told Killer he was now allowed to hunt for himself. He blinked his great eyes and looked bored.

Just as well he's in no hurry, I thought, because then he would have to be *tethered* to a perch like Vida was. I dreaded that because I didn't even like to put Lucky on a leash. I tried not to think about it.

Every day after I became a licensed *falconer,* the mail brought a new surprise: ads for training equipment, stuff from the Fish and Game Department, and finally an invitation to join a local hawking club. I didn't even know there was one in our city.

I asked Ron to go with me to see Old Mack again. I wanted to ask him about the club's invitation. Ron took one look at Mack and froze on the spot, but I wasn't afraid of him this time.

"Don't need a club," Mack muttered, tossing the invitation back to me.

"What are they for, then?" I asked.

"Competition." He spat out the word, then waved his hand. "Suit yourself." It was plain he didn't think much of organized hawking. I thought I'd better change the subject. Besides, I had lots of questions saved up to ask.

Ron's eyes bugged when we went outside to see Vida. She had a house of her own out back, if you want to call a little shed a house. But it looked like a palace to me because my bird had no house at all.

I started thinking, what will I do when Killer learns to fly? Then I would need training equipment like *jesses,* which are the tethers, *swivels,* some hoods, and leather gloves. I had no idea how much all this would cost, but it might as well be a million dollars because I didn't have it.

More and more I realized that raising a hawk was a full- time job. Every weekend I had to go to the hills to catch mice, lizards, and bugs to supply Killer with wild food. I had given up doing anything else.

On the way home from Mack's, Ron admitted, "He's not a bad guy when you get used to him. But I don't know how you ever got the nerve to go there in the first place."

"I was plenty scared, no kidding. But I like him now. He's so—so cool. I mean, he's got his head straight."

"Yeah," Ron agreed. "And living all by himself like that. Wait'll we tell Barney."

Barney's jaw dropped when I said the next day at school, "Thanks for telling me about Old Mack. He's really helping me with raising Killer."

For the first time I could remember, Barney and his friends had nothing to say.

Chapter 6

Killer was two months old, and I had just two or three weeks to do a thousand things before he started to fly at three months.

The pace was getting me down. Besides my paper route and school work, I had to spend several hours a day feeding and taking care of Killer, plus studying the falconry books. Every night I looked for answers to new questions that came up, and I went to see Mack as often as I could. I couldn't wait for school to let out.

I lost weight, too. Now I was really a skinny kid. I caught Mom looking at me one day. "Randy, are you feeling all right?"

"Sure, Mom, I'm fine." I tried to sound casual. She already knew I had given up playing basketball.

"You're getting attached to that bird, aren't you?" she asked slowly. Mom had a way of getting at the truth.

"Yeah, really," I grinned. "Have you seen him spread his wings? He's using them for balance when he walks. And have you noticed he's *fully summed?*"

"Oh, sure, all the time," she laughed. "What does that mean?"

I smiled. "Fully summed means he has all his feathers." I was talking like a trainer and didn't even realize it. The head

feathers had been the last to show. They made him look important. His spotted leg feathers fluttered in the breeze like ruffled
pants. His eyes were big yellow pools now with sharp black
centers. No doubt about it—he was outrageous.

Killer didn't like to be picked up anymore. I had to cup
his body and wings together, or he would spread his wings
and try to fly out of my hands. I tossed him in the air, and
he floated down to the grass with his wings out and panic
on his face.

I tried to show him about the flying business. I held out
my arms and flapped them a couple of times.

"Go, Rand, go." Leslee had come around the corner.

I felt silly. "Get lost," I said. "How else will Killer learn?
He hasn't got a mother."

"If I was a hawk," I told Ron one day, "I think I'd rather
fly in the open country and be free, wouldn't you?"

"I guess so," he said, "but if he did that you couldn't
hunt with him."

"I know." I looked away. I wondered if it was fair to
cage Killer just so I could test my skill as a hunter. I had
saved enough money for the jesses, but I still had the *mew,*
or house, to worry about.

Early June turned warm, and by the time school let out,

the weather was hot. Killer didn't like the heat at all. He
scooped out a hole in the ground under a bush and sat in
it with his beak parted. That sent me back to my books, and
I found out that a hawk should be offered a bath in summer-
time. Of course! Why hadn't I thought of that?

I filled a shallow pan with water and put Killer in the
middle of it. He gave me a couple of his upside down looks,
then stared at the water. He lifted one foot and made a stab
at the water with his *talons*. The splash surprised him so much
that he lost his balance and fell splat in the water.

That broke us up. Ron, Leslee, and I laughed so hard
we had to sit down. Killer scrambled to his feet and shook
his feathers, screaming in his high-pitched voice. He gave us
his most piercing stare, like he was scolding us for laughing.

Then he started drinking. He put his beak in the water
and tilted his head back to let the water run down his throat.
He made a couple more passes at the water with his feet and
decided he liked it. He splashed and drank until the water
was gone, then climbed out of the pan and walked away.

After that I kept the pan filled all the time and Killer
climbed in and out whenever he wanted to get a drink or cool
off. By this time he was wandering all over the yard, and
sometimes I had to hunt for him in the bushes.

Many people came to see Killer—friends, neighbors and even strangers. They "ohed" and "ahed" over him from a safe distance, and a few even got close enough to pet him. His fierce stare just about scared little kids to death. They hid behind their mothers and peeked out at the bird.

Killer loved it. He paraded around the yard and patio, showing off for the people. Ron laughed at him. "What a ham!"

I was so proud of him. Every day I planned to do something with him. I made a block perch out of a 4x4 post and padded the top end of it. Killer liked to sit on the perch and look around like he was posing for our national emblem.

I taught him to step backward onto my glove by pressing on the back of his legs. Hawks hate two things: stepping down and having the wind behind them. Even Lucky learned to tolerate Killer, but I wouldn't call them exactly buddies. Everything was going great.

Then it happened! One afternoon I found Killer lying on his side on the grass with one wing folded under his body.

Chapter 7

When I saw Killer lying on his side, a stab like a knife cut through me. Carefully, I set him on his feet. He toppled over and fell again, and I could see that one wing hung lower than the other, almost to the ground. He looked at me, his eyes pleading for help. Killer was in pain!

I carried him from the grass to the patio, found his old cardboard box in the garage, and made a new bed in a protected corner. I figured birds were like people, and they should be kept warm when they're hurt.

I raced to get the library books from my room, but I couldn't find anything about what to do for an injured wing. I was still reading when Leslee came out on the patio.

"Killer's been hurt. It's his wing," I said.

Her face fell. "How? What happened?"

"I don't know. I found him like that. Maybe he tried to fly and didn't make it."

She bent down to pet Killer's head and wiped away a tear.

"Watch him for me, Les, I'm going to see Mack."

I pedaled my bike as fast as my legs would go. Why didn't hermits have telephones? What if Mack wasn't home? I sighed out loud as I wheeled down Railroad Street and saw his bent figure hoeing in his garden. He grew all kinds of queer vegetables to eat.

"What's your hurry?" Mack looked up at me as I stood panting beside him. He never said hello.

I told him what had happened, talking fast and waving my arms. His faded green eyes watched me, even after I had finished.

"What do I do about a broken wing?" I asked.

He started to hoe again. "Probably not broken. Birds hurt their wings sometimes."

"How can I tell?" I followed him up the garden row.

"Can't really tell. Won't make any difference anyway. Keep him quiet for a while, and hope it heals."

"Oh, swell." I sat down on the ground and put my head on my knees. Mack worked for a few minutes in silence. Then he straightened up. "Want some lemonade?"

I walked behind him into the shack. He put out two jelly glasses on the table and filled them with chipped ice and lemonade from a pitcher. It was sour and sweet and cold. "Good," I said, wiping my mouth on my sleeve. You didn't have to be careful about manners at Mack's.

We drank without talking. You didn't have to talk at Mack's either, unless you wanted to. Pretty soon he got up and went out on the porch. He came back with something long wrapped in newspaper and handed it to me.

"Feed him some rhubarb, cooked in a little water. Good for what ails him."

"Oh, okay," I said and took the newspaper package. "How long should I keep him quiet?"

"Few days. Then try to make him use his wing." Mack looked straight at me. "You can do it."

I sighed and got up to go. "Thanks, Mack. What else should I give him?"

"Love." It sounded funny coming from the old man, but when I looked at him, I could see he meant it.

When I got home, it was almost dinnertime. Mom helped me boil the rhubarb, but Killer barely ate. A curtain of gloom settled over the house. Even Mom and Dad seemed worried.

The next day Killer was worse and refused to eat anything. For two more days, he huddled in his box, not even moving. I offered all his favorite foods with no luck. I had to force water down his throat with an eyedropper.

Killer didn't have symptoms of any regular hawk disease. I sat up late at night reading about *frounce, worms,* and *cramps,* but none of them fit Killer's sickness. His mouth was dry, and his tongue changed from healthy pink to a charcoal gray. He grew weaker and weaker.

It was Dad who first said it. We were talking that night at dinner about the trouble I was having getting Killer to eat. Dad listened and finally said, "Maybe Killer doesn't want to eat. Maybe he knows he can never fly and feed himself. He may be wiser than we are."

My stomach turned over. Maybe Dad was right. "And this might be nature's way of taking care of the wounded," I said to nobody in particular.

"Right—survival of the fittest, as they say," Dad added. He looked hard at me. "Rand, I guess you have to be prepared for the bad as well as the good in nature's scheme."

I thought about that. "It's funny, I've always figured that survival bit was a pretty neat system. But I never thought about the weak, the ones that had to die. Now it's different."

I forced Killer to swallow some of the rhubarb. At that point, it was probably the only thing keeping him alive. He looked pitiful—just a shadow of the proud bird he used to be—but the hardest thing to take was the sad look in his eyes.

Killer could move his wing a little bit, so I was pretty sure it wasn't broken. If I could only get him to eat!

I fell asleep that night determined not to let Killer die.

8

Chapter

Early the next morning, I jumped out of bed and ran to the patio to check on Killer. He was lying on his side, breathing heavily. I almost choked on the lump in my throat.

I dressed quickly and whistled for Lucky. He bounced around the corner, wagging his tail. Mom was busy in the kitchen.

"Mom, I'm going up in the hills for a while," I called to her. "I'll eat when I get home."

She turned the bacon over in the frying pan. She opened her mouth to say something, then closed it again when she saw the look on my face.

"All right, Randy. Don't be too long."

Good ol' Mom. At least she didn't yell at me for going off without breakfast. I wasn't hungry anyway. She probably knew I wanted to be alone to think. It was easier to think things over up in the hills.

Lucky and I ran the two blocks to the end of the street and crossed the field to the foothills. I slowed to a walk when the ground started getting steeper. Halfway to the top, Lucky shot ahead to chase a butterfly. When he was almost out of sight in the tall grass, I whistled, and he came tearing back and nearly knocked me over.

"Look where you're going, you dumb mutt," I shouted at him. His ears drooped and he fell into step behind me with his head down. I felt terrible.

I sat down on a rock and looked at him. "I'm sorry, Luck, honest. It's just that I'm so worried about Killer. He's going to die unless I can make him want to live." Lucky looked worried too. He wrinkled his forehead, and his brown eyes were sad with sympathy. The lump in my throat got bigger and bigger.

I sat on the rock for a long time, petting Lucky. He leaned against me and licked my hands, and I realized how I had neglected him lately.

All around me I saw signs of life. A caterpillar humped along on the ground, baby birds sang in the trees. Killer should be part of this, learning to fly in the blue sky with other birds. He should be growing up with courage and pride.

I thought about what Dad had said: the strong in nature survive. But what made them strong? Then I remembered Mack's saying, "You can do it." In his quiet way, he had tried to tell me something.

Suddenly I thought I knew the answer. *You can only be what you think you are. And if you think you are something long enough, that's what you become.*

Killer must not waste his life. I would make him want to live. I would make him think he could live. Maybe this was another wild idea, but at least I had to try.

I jumped up. "Come on, Luck. Race you home."

We made it home at a dead run. I couldn't get there fast enough. I went straight through the house to the patio and Killer's box.

I lifted the trembling bird out of his bed and set him firmly on the cement out in the bright sunshine. He blinked, stumbled, and fell. I stood him up again, but once more he fell. I kept trying, and I got a little rough with him, but after about the sixth time he wobbled, gained his balance, and stood alone.

Then I stretched out both wings and held them with my hands. When I let go, Killer folded his wings, and I noticed the injured wing drooped and seemed to be weaker than the other. I stretched them out again and again, forcing Killer to use his wings if only to fold them by his side.

I don't know why, but all at once I had to find out if Killer was going to make it. I took a deep breath and looked hard at him.

"Hey, Killer," I said sharply, "you're a tough hawk. Come on! WALK."

I couldn't believe my eyes. He actually seemed to understand what I had said. He took a couple of steps and when he started to fall, he spread his wings and balanced himself.

He stood still, blinking. Then, of all things, he stuck out his chest in his old pose. He looked outrageous.

"Mom, Les," I yelled, "come and see Killer." I rushed into the kitchen and cut up a handful of fresh meat. Mom followed me outside, and Leslee came on the run.

I forced Killer's beak open and put a tiny piece of meat on his tongue. Like he didn't know what else to do, he swallowed. Then while we all watched, he cocked his head and cheeped the happiest cheep I have ever heard. He ate another chunk of meat, and another.

I grinned. "You know, Killer is going to be okay."

"Randy, you did it, you did it!" Leslee jumped up and down. Lucky wagged his tail. Mom fished around in her pocket for a handkerchief.

It seemed like all my problems melted into those few steps of Killer's. He had faced his enemy and won. He was now master of his own life. It wasn't just a wild idea. It could be done!

Mom interrupted my thoughts. "How about some breakfast? We've got to put some meat on those bones this summer." She pinched my waist.

"Okay, Mom," I said. I'd eat just to humor her.

But when she put a steaming plate of bacon, eggs, and pancakes in front of me, I ate every bite.

Chapter 9

Killer mended fast. Once he had been shown that he could use his wing, he was a different bird. His appetite came back, and with it came his strength. It was nearly a week before he could eat by himself, and every day I had to help exercise the wing. But I didn't mind. He was getting well. That was the important thing.

I told Mack all about it. His eyes lit up like beacons when I told about getting Killer to use his wing and to walk. He didn't say much, but I knew he understood everything.

Before long Killer was tripping around the yard again, and fluttering out of my arms to the ground. He didn't favor his injured wing anymore and seemed stronger than ever. One day I took him to Mack's with me.

The old man looked the bird over from beak to tailfeathers. Then he tossed him into the air and watched him float to earth. He nodded, "You've done a good job, boy." The words were the best compliment I'd had in all my life.

Every day Killer got better with his wings. He used them with careless confidence as he moved.

And then one day, without any warning, Killer took off and flew. He ran a few steps on the grass, flapped his powerful

wings once, and lifted into the air. I yelled, and Mom, Dad, and Leslee came running. We stood and watched our hawk soar up over the back fence. He banked and drifted across the slope, then circled the yard above our heads.

We whooped and cheered. Dad laughed out loud and said, "You'd think he was Orville Wright."

I watched Killer against the sky and felt my throat tighten with pride and fear. I was afraid now that his days with me were numbered. Could I cage him, and did I really want to?

Killer's flying movements were jerky, but he sure was good at gliding. At last he came in low over the fence and made a perfect landing on the grass. He folded his wings and actually strutted across the patio. Talk about outrageous!

We all felt it immediately. There was a change in Killer. The family looked at me, and a weird feeling came over me. Right now, at this minute, I had to decide whether to train him or let him go free. Mom, Dad, and Les looked at me and waited.

It didn't take long. I stepped toward Killer and smiled. "That flying's great, huh, Killer? You were jerky today, but you'll do better next time, and you can fly anytime you want."

Killer would be free. I was surprised at how glad I felt now that I had decided. And I knew it was the right choice for Killer. He was not the kind of bird for captivity. We had needed each other for a while, but now we could both go on alone.

I was afraid to look at Dad. Would he think I hadn't finished this project either? But when I did look at him, he was smiling. No, he was beaming.

"Good decision, Rand. I'd say setting Killer free would be a perfect finish. Don't you think so, Mother?" I knew Mom agreed, just because of the way she was looking at me.

The next few days were really exciting. Flying was like a new toy to Killer, and he was almost always airborne. He learned something new every day—different takeoffs and fast landings. No question about it, he had style.

Everybody came to see him. He was the talk of the neighborhood. Even Barney Cooper came over one day. I almost dropped my teeth when I saw him. He watched Killer fly and even asked to hold him.

"He's neat, Randy," Barney said. "Everybody's talking about him. Raising a hawk's really something, even for a skinny kid." But he laughed when he said it, and I laughed too. The funny part was I didn't mind any more.

"Got to go. Are you coming out for basketball next year?"

"Sure thing," I said. Why not? Varsity basketball might be my next project.

Even though Killer flew most of the day, he came back to our yard to sleep at night, and I still put out his food. But I suspected that he had begun to hunt for himself.

Mack summed it up, "He was born to kill." That was the day I asked Mack to come over for dinner because Mom and Dad wanted to meet him. He looked pleased, but he only said, "Maybe. Maybe sometime."

Then, as we all expected, Killer disappeared. He had gone free to his natural home. Maybe he found a mate or joined a group of migrating hawks. I hope so.

That was three weeks ago. His perch still stands in the yard, and I look up in the sky whenever I'm outside, hoping to see that familiar outline against the blue. I really believe he'll be back, if only for a visit.

I do miss him. But wherever Killer is, he carries part of me with him. I hope he's safe and I want to thank him for a very special gift.

You see, Killer gave me something few human beings ever have—a true friendship with a wild creature.

Glossary/Index

About the Author and Illustrator

A California resident, Mrs. Bonnie Robison has three loves besides her family: sports, nature, and writing.

Killer, The Outrageous Hawk is based on the experiences of the Robison family of Hacienda Heights, California. An abandoned baby hawk actually grew up, survived, and taught Randy Robison and his family a great deal about hawks and falconry.

Rob Sprattler is a free lance artist who has illustrated ads, books, record album covers, and materials for children's TV shows. A graduate of The Art Center College of Design at Los Angeles, he lives in Southern California where he and his wife enjoy skiing, motorcycle touring, and traveling to Mexico.